Croc on the Rock

Marion Clark and Tanya Fenton

The giant croc, he sat on his rock
And watched the river go by,
Until a hippo he saw slip in for a swim
As he lazily opened one eye.

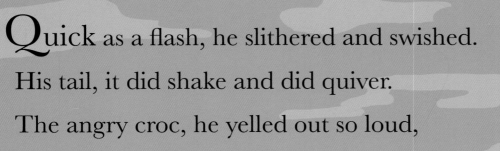

Quick as a flash, he slithered and swished.

His tail, it did shake and did quiver.

The angry croc, he yelled out so loud,

"Will you get out of my river?"

"GET OUT OF MY RIVER!"

Yelled the croc on the rock,

"I'll eat you for my tea."

The giant croc, he sat on his rock
And watched the river go by,
Until a tiger he saw slip in for a splash
As he lazily opened one eye.

Furious again, he stood on his rock
And thumped 'til the water did shiver.
The angry croc, he yelled out so loud,

"Will you get out of my river?"

"**GET OUT OF MY RIVER!**"
Yelled the croc on the rock,
"I'll eat you for my tea."

"**GET OUT OF MY RIVER!**"
Yelled the croc on the rock,
"It's only meant for **me!**"

The giant croc, he sat on his rock
And watched the river go by,
Until an elephant he saw dip in for a drink
As he lazily opened one eye.

Mad as could be, he crept from his rock,
Diving in with barely a sliver.

He swam right up to the elephant's trunk,

"Will you get out of my river?"

"GET OUT OF MY RIVER!"

Yelled the croc on the rock,

"I'll eat you for my tea."

"GET OUT OF MY RIVER!"

Yelled the croc on the rock,

"It's only meant for **me!**"

The croc on the rock was mad as could be,

His tail, it did shake and did quiver.

He stomped on his rock and yelled out so loud ...

"Everyone out of my River!"

All the animals ran to the side of the banks.

There were turtles, snakes and a rat,

A bison, a hog and a hopping great frog,

A cheetah, a deer

and a bat.

The giant croc, he swam all day,

Then tired he snored through his nap.

He lazed and bathed and basked 'til dusk,

And he yawned with a snapity snap.

Morning came; no bustle or hustle,

No splishing, no splashing, no sound.

The croc on the rock was missing his friends ...

... he was lonely now, he found.

He was miserable now, and he cried so hard

That his body did shake and did shiver,

"I'm sorry to have been so mean to my friends.

Could you please all

come back to the river?"

Back came the animals ready to play,
Turtles, snakes and a rat,
A bison, a hog
    and a hopping great frog,
A cheetah, a deer and a bat.

Now the giant croc, he sits on his rock

And watches the river go by.

As animals come for a drink or a swim,

He welcomes them in and says ...

"Hi!"

Published by
Hogs Back Books
The Stables
Down Place
Hogs Back
Guildford GU3 1DE
www.hogsbackbooks.com
Text copyright © 2012 Marion Clark
Illustrations copyright © 2012 Tanya Fenton
The moral right of Marion Clark to be identified as the author
and of Tanya Fenton to be identified as the illustrator of this work has been asserted.
First published in Great Britain in 2013 by Hogs Back Books Ltd.

Printed in Singapore
ISBN: 978-1-907432-14-9
British Library Cataloguing-in-Publication Data.
A catalogue record for this book is available from the British Library.
1 3 5 4 2